DISNEY

Before the Story

Anita's
PUPPY TALE

BY
TESSA ROEHL

ILLUSTRATED BY
ARIANNA REA

DISNEY PRESS

Los Angeles • New York

For Oliver and Bruley
—T.R.

Special thanks to Cathryn Mchugh

Based on the book THE HUNDRED AND ONE DALMATIANS
BY DODIE SMITH Published by The Viking Press.

First Paperback Edition, April 2021

10 9 8 7 6 5 4 3 2 1

Lexile: 770L

ISBN 978-1-368-06207-7

FAC-029261-21057

Library of Congress Control Number: 2020933582

Printed in the United States of America

For more Disney Press fun, visit www.disneybooks.com

Chapter 1
The Headmistress

There was a skip in Anita's step as she walked to her dormitory at Dahlington Academy for Girls. After two weeks at boarding school, she'd just received her first piece of mail: a letter from her mum. Her fingers clutched the envelope, itching to tear it open.

Beatrice, Anita's roommate, was reading on her bed when Anita entered their room.

"Lovely day outside," Anita said to Beatrice. "Care to explore the grounds later?"

Without looking up from her book, Beatrice responded with a slight shake of her head. Her corkscrew curls hung like a curtain over her face, further separating her from Anita. Everything frightened Beatrice, from Anita's old stuffed rabbit, to the sounds of other students passing in the hall, to her own reflection in the mirror above the wardrobe. Beatrice's brush-off was no surprise, as Anita's short time at Dahlington had been filled with similar failed efforts to make friends.

When Anita tried to start a conversation

with her tablemates over lunch on the first day, she'd immediately been shushed by the student aide who patrolled the dining hall. One rainy day after classes, she'd set up her easel and canvas in the common room, hoping other girls would stop by, perhaps to chat about her painting, or even just to sit in a nearby chair and study. But no one did.

Anita sat down at her desk with a sigh. She opened the letter and began to read. Her mum, who had attended the same school when she was young, wrote that she was eager to hear whether Anita was having as great a time at Dahlington as

she'd had as a girl. In the letter's pages, her mum recalled the school where she had made all her lifelong friends and formed her dearest memories. It was the same dreamy Dahlington Academy story she had told Anita all her life. But one thing was for certain: it was *not* the Dahlington Academy Anita had been enrolled in for the past two weeks.

The location was the same, in the postcard-perfect countryside. The history was the same, as one of the most esteemed boarding schools for girls in all of England. And the name was the same; Anita had checked the iron placard in the great hall several times just to be sure. But the school Anita's mum described had changed.

Peeling paint and scuffed floors replaced the gleaming marble and polished wood of her mum's memories. Instead of bands of merry girls filling the halls with laughter, solitary students ventured out of their dormitories only for classes or meals. Rather than lively, inspirational debates in the classroom, there were dull, dry lessons straight from the ancient textbooks. And this stricter, bleaker school came complete with a thick book of rules handed out to incoming students on their first day.

Through it all Anita had done her best to stay positive. She tried to keep a smile on her face, no matter how dreary things seemed. But forcing happiness on the outside hadn't been enough to change the way she felt on the inside. Anita was lonely and miserable.

Tears began to fall from Anita's eyes as she read her mum's words. Somehow, she'd let herself hope that the letter would be an explanation of why the school was so cold now, instructions with the right thing to say or do to bring back the wonderful academy of her mum's childhood.

Just as she was about to toss the letter into the rubbish bin, Anita spotted a postscript at the bottom of the last page, under her mum's signature: *P.S. Don't forget to sign up for one of Dahlington's clubs! The tennis club was where I made some of my best friends.*

Anita bolted upright, wiping her eyes. No one had mentioned clubs since Anita arrived at the school. She wondered: Was this the answer? Would she find her true friends and make memories in a club?

She checked the clock. There was a couple of hours left before dinner, enough time to speak to the Headmistress. She folded up the letter, put it in her blazer pocket, and grabbed her coat.

"Beatrice," Anita said, "I'm going to speak to the Headmistress about joining a club. Would you like to come along?"

Beatrice looked up at Anita in wide-eyed alarm. *"Headmistress?"* she warbled. She shook her head and returned to her reading.

Anita shrugged and set out for the Headmistress's office, alone as ever.

The hallway outside the Headmistress's office was deserted and eerily quiet. Anita was nervous about speaking to the head of the school on her own. She wished she had a friend, even terrified Beatrice, by her side. Patting the letter in her pocket for courage, Anita took a deep breath and knocked on the door.

"Enter." The voice inside sounded faint and tired. Anita turned the knob and let herself in.

The Headmistress's office was as gloomy as the rest of Dahlington. The furniture, lamps, photographs, and wall hangings were all draped in large sheets of fabric. Anita wondered if perhaps the Headmistress was terrified of dust; that might explain the odd coverings. The woman herself, her dull

brown hair swept up in a bun, sat at her desk, riffling through the pages of a photo album.

"Excuse me, ma'am," Anita began.

"Mmm," was the only response the Headmistress gave. She didn't look up.

"My name is Anita," Anita continued. "I'm a first-year student, and I was wondering if there are any clubs here I could join. I wasn't sure who else to ask, and—"

"Clubs?" the Headmistress asked, still engrossed in the photos.

"Yes, ma'am," Anita said. "My mum was in the tennis club. She loved being on the Dahlington team back in her day."

"The tennis club is gone," the Headmistress replied, turning a page in her album.

"It is?" Anita frowned. "Well, I'm more interested in an art club, anyway—"

"There is no art club."

"Theater?"

"No."

"Poetry?"

"No."

"Chess?"

"No."

Anita was getting discouraged. "What clubs *do* you have?"

The Headmistress sighed and finally lifted her eyes from the photographs. "We only have one club. You ought to speak to Cruella about it."

"Cruella?" Anita asked.

"Cruella De Vil, my student aide," the Headmistress said. "She's in the year above you. In fact, she's probably in club room 101 right now."

"Thank you," Anita said. The Headmistress cast her gaze back down. Anita could tell the visit was over. She left the office and closed the door behind her, heading off to find Cruella De Vil and, hopefully, some trace of the Dahlington her mother had once known.

Chapter 2
The Fashion Club

Anita wandered the school halls, looking for Cruella. Eventually, down a tucked-away wing of the first floor, Anita found a classroom with an open door, its light spilling into the otherwise dark hallway. The doorplate read *Club Room 101*, though the second *1* was upside down.

She took a cautious step inside. Scattered around the room were top-of-the-line sewing machines. Strewn atop the desks and chairs were yards of fabric in all kinds of colors and textures: purple taffeta, ivory silk, tangerine wool, emerald-green velvet. In the back were several dress forms, each draped with a different outrageous ensemble. On one hung a burgundy pantsuit speckled with swirls of lavender beads and draped with a glimmering silver cape. On another was a shocking-green hooded minidress trimmed in gold and brown fringe. Anita might have wondered if she was in the right place if it wasn't for what covered the walls: old club rosters and photos were tacked up everywhere. But curiously, each one had a large red X slashed through it.

The room appeared to be empty of any club members. But then a girl, crouching, emerged from behind one of the dress forms, her back to Anita as she poked and prodded at the fabric in front of her.

"Excuse me, are you Cruella?" Anita waved her hand shyly as the older student turned around.

The girl's mouth was clamped shut, holding the pins she had been using to adjust the fabric on the mannequin. Her hair was a mane of chaos, half black and half white, as wild as her giant, ferocious eyes. Those eyes narrowed slightly when she saw Anita. She spit the pins out of her mouth and

stabbed them into the dress form.

"Yes," she answered, her voice calm in spite of the frenzied scene. "I'm Cruella. Cruella De Vil."

Anita realized she had seen Cruella before. There wasn't anyone else in Dahlington with that hairstyle. Cruella was the student aide who patrolled the dining hall at mealtimes, enforcing table manners and shutting down attempts at socializing. "My name is Anita," she said. "The Headmistress said I should speak to you about clubs?"

"Clubs?" Cruella pursed her lips, smoothing strands of hair away from her face.

"Yes," Anita said. "I was hoping to join an art club. I love to paint, but—"

"There is no art club," Cruella said. She smirked and began to take slow, slinking steps toward Anita. "All the clubs have been disbanded. Except mine, that is."

Anita felt like a mouse under a cat's stare. After two weeks of feeling invisible, she was uneasy having someone watch her so closely. "What is this club?" Anita asked.

"It's a fashion club, Anita darling," Cruella said, grabbing one of the pieces of fabric from a nearby desk and tossing it around her neck like a boa. "You're welcome to join."

"I don't know how to sew," Anita said, eyeing one of the contraptions on the desk closest to her. It was a piece of machinery so complex Anita wondered if she'd need a university degree just to turn it on.

Cruella tipped back her head and cackled. "You wouldn't be sewing, oh no." She dabbed tears of laughter from her eyes. "There are so many other ways you can contribute. You can take notes on my ideas; you can be my alternate dress form; you can hold the pincushion . . . Oh, the list goes on and on for how I could use you!"

It sounded like Anita would be Cruella's assistant rather than another member of the club. "That's awfully nice of you to offer. Where are the other members?"

"It's just me," Cruella said.

Anita wondered what made this a club and not just Cruella's hobby. "But why is it just you? What happened to everyone else? What happened to the other clubs?"

Cruella shrugged. "Not everyone can keep up with the fashion club, Anita. All the other clubs lost their funding."

"All of them?" Anita asked.

"Things happen," Cruella continued. "Clubs break rules . . . members stop paying their dues . . . people lose interest. I suppose I'm just the only survivor."

"What would it take for someone to start a new club? Do you know?" Anita asked.

"Of course I know," Cruella snapped. Then she collected herself, unfurled the makeshift boa, and placed it back on the desk. "You need five shillings in dues plus any additional funds for club supplies, the signatures of at least five other interested students, an official meeting place, and, finally, the approval and permission of the Headmistress."

"That's all, is it?" Anita said sarcastically.

Cruella didn't seem to get the joke. She turned back to the dress form.

Anita sighed. She couldn't even get her own roommate to speak to her. How would she ever get another five students on her side?

"Thank you anyway," Anita said to Cruella. On her way out of the club room, Anita paused to study one of the photographs on the wall. It had a red X through it, like all the others, but Anita could still make out most of the image. It was an old tennis club photo. And there, on the right, with a familiar wide smile and glasses, was Anita's mum. Anita reached out to touch the picture. This was the Dahlington her mum loved, and it was just out of Anita's grasp, trapped in a photo from the past.

As Anita studied the image, she realized she didn't recognize the location. In the background, behind the girls, was a small tidy structure.

"Cruella," Anita said, "in this tennis club photo, what is the building in the background?"

"That's the old equipment shed," Cruella answered from her dress form. It sounded like her mouth was full of pins again. "You should go find it. Maybe it will inspire you for your little art club." Cruella cackled at the idea. As Anita left club room 101, Cruella's laughter continued to echo through the dingy hallway behind her.

Dahlington Academy's exterior was in much the same neglected condition as the interior: the grass was overgrown, the hedges needed trimming, and pockets of weeds dotted the landscape. Anita figured that the equipment shed would be near the tennis courts, which were all the way on the outskirts of the school grounds. She wasn't quite sure why she wanted to find it, but seeing the photograph of her mum made her feel drawn to it.

When Anita reached the courts, she saw the shed right away. The bright paint had faded, the shutters hung askew, and part of the roof had collapsed. Nevertheless, Anita went in.

The inside of the shed was an even sorrier sight. Cobwebs hung in the corners, dust coated every surface, and the windows were so dirty they hardly let any light in. The place also seemed to have become a dumping ground for whatever students and teachers wanted to forget. Broken chairs lay on their sides, rusted gardening tools hung on the walls, and random bits of sports equipment were scattered everywhere.

It was a fitting end to Anita's afternoon. It felt like someone had painted a big red X over all the hope she'd felt after reading her mum's letter.

As Anita turned to leave, she tripped over a stack of books, falling and skinning her knee. "Ouch!" she squealed.

A rustle came from the other side of the shed.

Anita scrambled back to her feet. If there were rats in the shed, she didn't want to meet them. She had just reached the door when she heard a cry that pierced her heart—a cry for help.

Despite her fear of what could be lurking in the shadows, Anita crept toward the noise. She moved aside some boxes and lifted an old book. There, underneath, panting and wagging its tail, was a Dalmatian puppy.

Chapter 3
Perdita

"**W**here did you come from?" Anita asked, noticing the puppy wasn't wearing a collar. Her black-and-white-spotted fur was dirty, and Anita could see the faint outline of her ribs. She wondered how the pup had been surviving in this wretched storage shed.

Anita held out her hand. The puppy approached cautiously, sniffing Anita's fingers. Seeming to instantly decide she was a friend, the dog leapt forward to lick Anita's face. Anita laughed, scooping her up and cuddling her tight. "I'm here now. I'm here," she cooed.

Dahlington students weren't allowed to keep pets; Anita didn't have to check the enormous rule book to know that. But the poor thing couldn't stay in the shed.

"Do you want to come to my room?" Anita asked the puppy.

"Woof!" the puppy answered in a delighted bark.

"Shhh." Anita pressed a finger to her lips. "You can't make noise, or someone will find out." She scratched the puppy behind

the ears. "Now, what shall we call you?"

Anita picked up the book that had been on top of the puppy and flipped through the pages. Her eyes stopped on the first name she found: *Perdita*.

"'Perdita,'" she read aloud. "Do you like that?"

The puppy nuzzled into Anita's neck. It seemed she did.

"Stay quiet, then, Perdita." Anita tucked the puppy inside her coat, shielding her from view as she headed back toward the school.

Anita made it to the dormitory and up to her floor without encountering another soul. Perdita stayed quiet and calm, nestled inside Anita's coat. On the walk over, Anita had tried to think of how she could convince Beatrice to let her keep Perdita in their room. In a way, Anita hoped Beatrice might ignore Perdita the same way she ignored her.

When Anita entered, Beatrice was huddled up on her bed as usual, staring at the open book in her lap.

"Beatrice?" Anita asked. Beatrice raised

her eyes slowly. "Hello," Anita said. "I don't want you to be frightened, but I've got something to show you."

Anita unwrapped her coat and revealed the puppy in her arms. Perdita had fallen fast asleep and was snoozing with soft snores. Beatrice's hands flew to her cheeks in surprise, her book forgotten.

"Please don't tell anyone," Anita said. "She was living in the shed out behind the school."

Without a word, Beatrice reached out her arms toward Perdita.

"You'd like to hold her?" Anita asked. Beatrice nodded. Anita was surprised, but she placed the sleeping puppy in Beatrice's arms. Beatrice hugged Perdita to her chest. Then she dissolved into tears.

Anita was taken aback by Beatrice's sudden outburst. The tears startled Perdita as well, waking the puppy up from her nap. Beatrice continued to wail, and Perdita stretched her neck to find the source of the sound. She put her front paws on Beatrice's shoulder and nuzzled her face until Beatrice started laughing. "That tickles!" Beatrice said, giggling and sniffling as the puppy continued to lick away her tears.

Anita kneeled in front of the bed. "Are you all right?" she asked Beatrice.

Beatrice sighed and settled Perdita onto her lap. "I don't know," Beatrice said. "Something about this school. It's not what I thought it was going to be. It's . . . it's . . ." Beatrice searched for the right word.

"Terrible?" Anita suggested.

"Yes!" Beatrice exclaimed. "You think so, too?"

"Of course I do!" Anita replied.

"But you seem so positive and rather happy," Beatrice said. "I thought I was the only one feeling like an outcast."

"Beatrice, this school is full of gloom and

doom," Anita said. "No one smiles. No one talks. My mum always told me stories about how wonderful her Dahlington years were. Clearly something has happened since then to make it awful." It was a relief for Anita to finally tell someone the way she'd been feeling for the past two weeks.

Beatrice nodded. "I was so afraid to face the loneliness, I tried to pretend it wasn't happening." Beatrice watched Perdita, who was batting her book pages back and forth, playing. "But this puppy made me think about my dogs at home, and suddenly I felt so homesick it was like I couldn't keep it inside anymore, and . . ." Beatrice pointed at her teary eyes, wiping them with her shirtsleeve.

"I know what you mean," Anita said. "I tried to do something about it today by joining a club, and it didn't quite go as planned." Anita told Beatrice all about her afternoon, from her mum's letter, to her visit with the Headmistress, to her encounter with Cruella, and, finally, to her discovery of Perdita.

"Well, let's start an art club!" Beatrice said. "That was what you really wanted to join, right?"

"Yes, but how can we?" Anita asked. "We have to find other members in a school where no one talks—not to mention raise all that money for the club fee and supplies."

"I'm sure there are more girls like us, looking for a place to belong," Beatrice said. "And we can raise the money with fundraisers!"

Anita couldn't believe this enthusiastic and lively girl was the same one who had been cowering on her bed for the past two weeks. "I'm willing to give it a try if you are." Anita grinned.

"We'll start our recruiting at dinner," Beatrice said. She picked up Perdita and gave her a kiss. "Won't we?" she asked the puppy. Perdita yapped her agreement.

The two came up with a plan for spreading the message about their club. As they chatted, they settled Perdita into her new home. They wiped her dirty fur clean and set her up with a bed of blankets and Anita's stuffed rabbit to cuddle. Anita was relieved that Beatrice was already as head over heels in love with Perdita as she was. She was confident her roommate wouldn't spill her puppy secret any time soon.

Chapter 4
Supper Plans

At mealtime, Dahlington students were allowed to speak to one another only when it directly related to their meal, such as when they needed to ask another student for a dish or a utensil. Cruella patrolled the dining hall to enforce the rules. Anita and Beatrice had decided the quickest and best way to spread their recruitment message was to pass notes under the cover of their normal dinner activity. They just had to do it without Cruella noticing.

Dining hall seats were assigned according to dormitories. Anita was always seated across from Beatrice at a table they shared with four neighbors from their floor. As they sat down, Anita studied the other girls. Next to Beatrice and Anita were Claire and Madeline. Claire had short red hair and wore a different hat every day. Hats were not allowed as part of the official Dahlington uniform, and Anita admired that Claire wore them anyway. Madeline had long dark brown hair and kind eyes, and her mouth often formed into a small smile that looked to Anita like she was trying to put on a brave face. Rounding out the table were Lucy and Penelope, who appeared every bit the opposite of each other. Lucy was short with smooth blond hair and fair features, while Penelope was tall with dark hair and eyes.

The meals at Dahlington were usually bland and unenjoyable. That night's dinner was no different: the kitchen staff set down a large bowl of lumpy mashed potatoes, a tray of dried-out ham, and a platter of limp vegetables. The ham would at least make a good supper for Perdita, and Anita wrapped some in a napkin and put it in her pocket.

The girls dished up their food. Anita

and Beatrice waited for the clamor of silverware and plates to die down. Then Anita began with Claire: "Yes, Claire," she said abruptly. "Here's the salt." Anita pushed the salt shaker toward Claire with a folded note underneath. On the piece of paper was written: *Meet in Beatrice and Anita's room after lights-out. Important. Starting a club. Pass around.*

Claire stared at the salt shaker, confused.

"Psst," Beatrice whispered to Claire, and pointed at the note.

Claire finally saw the scrap of paper and picked it up, scanning quickly for Cruella before unfolding it. She read the message

and passed it to Madeline. Madeline read the note and passed it to Lucy, who read it and passed it to Penelope. Penelope read the note, sighed, and went back to pushing her food around on her plate.

Beatrice and Anita looked at each other. Not one of their neighbors seemed very excited about the message. *We tried,* Anita mouthed to her roommate, shrugging.

Frowning, Beatrice got up and snatched the note from Penelope.

"Hey!" Penelope said before realizing she shouldn't speak. A few students turned around, but Cruella was on the far side of the dining hall and didn't seem to notice.

Beatrice pulled a pen from her pocket, scribbled on the other side of the paper, then shoved it in the middle of the table so all the girls could see.

Claire, Madeline, Lucy, and Penelope peered down at the note. Their eyes bulged in surprise. Written in bold capital letters was *WE HAVE A PUPPY IN OUR ROOM.*

The girls looked up at Anita and Beatrice, brimming with delight. Their faces were full of questions, all of which would have to wait until later. Beatrice's direct approach hadn't been the plan, but it had broken

Dahlington's cold spell over the students at the table for now. The six girls smiled at one another, sharing nods of agreement.

That evening, after lights-out, the other girls snuck over to Anita and Beatrice's room. The group gathered on the floor, where Madeline, Claire, Lucy, and Penelope oohed and aahed over the puppy. Perdita relished the attention.

The girls peppered Anita with questions about where Perdita had been found and what Anita planned to do with her.

"She *has* to stay here," Madeline said after Anita had finished explaining.

"This is her home!" Lucy added.

"She couldn't have picked a nicer one?" Penelope joked.

"Well, even if the rest of the school is miserable," Anita said, "this room can be a happy place." Perdita yelped in agreement.

The girls all shushed the puppy at once, then dissolved into giggles.

"But that's also why we're here," Beatrice said. "To create another happy place."

"Right," Anita said. She told the other girls about their plan to start an art club and what she'd learned from the Headmistress and Cruella.

"Cruella De Vil?" Claire said. "She asked

me to join her fashion club, too."

"She did?" Anita replied.

Claire nodded. "She came up to me one day, asking about my hats. My father is a hatmaker in London. She was fawning all over them, and she told me if I gave her my hats, she might let me into her club. I didn't like the sound of that, so I said no."

"You told her no? She seems so scary, though," Beatrice said.

"I did," Claire continued. "And then, just a day later, the Headmistress found me and told me that hats weren't allowed as part of the uniform. It was strange timing, since I'd been wearing them every day until then and no one had said anything."

"What did you do?" Madeline asked, noting that Claire was still wearing a hat. A fine tweed newsboy cap, at that.

Claire shrugged. "I got a note from my father giving me special permission, and no one bothered me again. I've been getting a lot of glares from Cruella, though."

Perdita scampered from Lucy's lap into the center of the room. She grabbed the plush rabbit in her mouth, despite its being as large as she was, and started

shaking it. That made the girls giggle
again.

"So, what do you say about the art club?"
Anita asked the group.

"I'm definitely in," Claire said.

"Me too," the rest chimed in.

"Great!" Anita shouted, then covered
her mouth, smiling.

Beatrice took out a pad of paper. "First
thing is fundraising so we can pay five
shillings to the school and get some art
supplies. Let's write down some ideas."

The girls brainstormed as they played with Perdita. Their ideas ranged from serious, to silly, to brilliant. When her face started hurting from laughing, Anita realized that this was the first time she'd really smiled since she'd arrived at Dahlington. It wasn't the brave smile she'd been wearing as her Dahlington armor, but a true smile. A grin she couldn't fight off if she tried—not that she would want to.

By the time Claire, Madeline, Lucy, and Penelope said good night and snuck back to their own rooms, Anita and Beatrice had a list of fundraising ideas and a plan for the next day.

Chapter 5
A Close Call

Breakfast the next morning was better than any meal Anita had eaten since she arrived at boarding school, and it wasn't because of the food. She was finally catching a glimpse of her mum's Dahlington: a place to make friends, do new things, and learn more about herself.

The new art club—or the Arties, as they now called themselves—had decided that their first fundraiser would be a cake stall where they could sell homemade baked goods. Madeline, whose parents owned a bakery in London, was taking the lead. Beatrice suggested asking Dahlington's headmistress to let them use the kitchens and ingredients from the pantries. While they probably would not be able to make enough pastries to earn the five shillings in dues, it would be a good start.

After finishing breakfast, they tried to go talk to the Headmistress about gaining access to the kitchens, but when they knocked on her door, there was no answer. Anita suggested they ask Cruella.

So they walked back to the dining hall to find Cruella just then sitting down to eat.

"What do we say?" Madeline whispered as they approached.

"We simply ask about the kitchens," Anita answered. "We say exactly what we want to do."

"She'd better not comment on my hat," Claire muttered.

Anita knew Cruella didn't have the warmest reputation at the school, and she'd certainly been unusual during their brief encounter. But Anita also understood that Dahlington didn't bring out the best in people, so she didn't want to judge Cruella too harshly.

Anita cleared her throat. "Cruella?" The older girl glanced up from her breakfast to see the whole art club watching her.

Cruella's mouth peeled back into a sly grin. "Anita, darling, hello! Have you reconsidered my fashion club?"

"Actually, Cruella, you've inspired me to start my own club," Anita said. "An art club."

"Is that so?" One of Cruella's thin, dark eyebrows arched up in amusement.

"We want to have a fundraiser to earn money," Beatrice said.

"But we need some help from the

Dahlington staff," Anita said. She relayed the Arties' plans to Cruella.

"So you're going to raise funds?" Cruella drummed her fingers against her pale cheek. "Not just for your dues, but all your art supplies, too?"

"That's the idea," Beatrice said.

Cruella cackled. She seemed strangely delighted. "How tremendous," Cruella said. "I'll grant you permission to use the kitchens."

"You will?" the Arties said together.

"Can you?" Penelope asked.

"Of course I can," Cruella retorted. "The Headmistress has other matters to deal with. As her student aide, I can oversee these minor bits of red tape."

"Really? Do we need a permission slip or any-thing?" Claire asked.

Cruella glared at Claire. "My word is as good as any silly scrap of paper."

The Arties looked at each other and shrugged. "Thank you so much," Anita said to Cruella.

"I'm looking forward to the cake stall, girls. Hope you earn big." Cruella winked.

The Arties said goodbye to Cruella, leaving her to her breakfast.

"See? She's not bad," Anita said as they exited the dining hall.

"Perhaps not," Claire said. "Maybe she just really liked my hats."

"I don't know," Penelope said. "I've heard that she's a bit of a schemer."

"As long as her scheming lets us make enough money to start our club," Beatrice said, "it's fine by me!"

"Shall we go look up recipes in the library?" Madeline asked. "The only one I've got memorized is for scones, and we'll need more options than that."

"I'm supposed to meet a girl from my

English class to study, but I'd much rather look for recipes!" Beatrice said.

"You all go ahead," Anita said. She lowered her voice to a whisper. "I've got to go feed Perdita."

The Arties bid Anita goodbye, and they agreed to meet in the kitchens after dinner to start baking.

Inside the dorm room, Perdita was napping on her bed of blankets in a beam of sunlight. Not wanting to disturb the puppy's rest, Anita set aside the food she'd snuck away from breakfast. She decided to use the time to write her mum a letter.

As Anita set down a piece of stationery on her desk and uncapped her favorite fountain pen, she suddenly felt like she might burst with all the good news she had to share. The words flowed from her faster than her hand could write. She told her mum about each one of her new friends. That led into the art club she was starting and all the activities and fun that would come from it. Anita decided not to mention Perdita for now.

As she neared the end of the letter, Anita was interrupted by the piercing sound of a whistle. She peered out the open window above her desk. A group of boys was playing soccer down the road at Dapperton, the boys' school. Anita heard toenails scrabbling on the wood floor behind her. Perdita had been startled awake and was running around the small room.

The whistle sounded again. Perdita sprang onto Anita's bed, then leapt onto the desk. The puppy thrust her snout at the window and began to bark.

"No!" Anita cried. She quickly shut the window. Perdita still woofed and howled, excited by the sound of the whistle.

"Shhh, Perdy, shhh." Anita pleaded with the puppy to quiet down. Another whistle blew, muffled this time by the window, but Perdita still heard it. She thought the whistle meant it was time to play, and she kept trying to get back to the window. Anita began to sing, hoping her voice would distract Perdita. To Anita's relief, after a few rounds of "Mary Had a Little Lamb," Perdita finally calmed down. Anita continued to sing nursery rhymes until the soccer game was over. Eventually, Perdita settled back down in her bed of blankets to nap.

Anita was concerned. What if Perdita heard a noise like that when Anita wasn't there to soothe her? What if she barked and someone discovered her? Anita couldn't bear to have Perdita taken away. Not when she had been the first happy thing Anita had found at the school and had been the key to unlocking her new friendships. Anita would just have to be more careful.

Chapter 6
Kitchen Duty

That evening after dinner, the Arties entered the kitchen. Anita opened her book bag and let Perdita out from hiding. Perdita trotted around the unfamiliar room, sniffing all the new smells.

The girls set to work with Madeline in charge. Along with the scones, they were making fudge, oatmeal walnut biscuits, apple tarts, and small multicolored cakes.

Some were white with dots of chocolate icing, as a secret nod to Perdita.

It was glorious fun for the girls, getting their hands sticky with chocolate, their clothes covered in flour, and their faces dusted with sugar—all the while with Perdita there to play at their feet. Despite some burned biscuits, everything was going according to plan. The smell of baked sweets filled the kitchen as the scones, tarts, and biscuits cooled on a counter. The girls were just getting started on the fudge and cakes when there was a sound at the door.

The Arties froze. Perdita was licking a drop of butter next to Lucy's shoe. Anita grabbed the puppy and frantically searched for a hiding place. Settling on a large cupboard, Anita gently put Perdita inside. She had just closed the doors when in walked Cruella De Vil.

"Hello, darlings," Cruella purred as she observed the scene in the kitchen. Madeline was melting chocolate on the stove while Lucy unwrapped butter, Claire measured sugar, Beatrice cracked eggs, Penelope washed dishes, and Anita stood in front of the closed cupboard. Everyone paused to watch Cruella. "Go on," Cruella urged. "Don't stop what you're doing on my account. I just wanted to see how your little bakery is getting on."

"Everything's coming along smoothly, Cruella," Anita said, hoping that the older girl wouldn't get any closer. Anita heard a tiny whimper from the cupboard and faked a giant sneeze to cover it up. *"Achoo!"*

Cruella shot Anita a disgusted look. "Are you sick, Anita? Should you be in the kitchen baking if you're ill?"

Anita waved her off. "It's just all the flour flying around, tickling my nose."

Another whimper came from the cupboard, and Lucy, who was closest to Anita, blurted out, "Would you like to taste something, Cruella? A biscuit, perhaps?"

Cruella walked to the cooling baked

goods and studied them. "I don't eat sweets," she said. "I don't see the point."

"They taste delicious," Penelope said. "That's the point."

Cruella shrugged. "How much will you sell them for?"

Perdita let out another muffled cry, and Beatrice spoke loudly to cover it up: "One ha'penny each for the biscuits."

"Interesting," Cruella said. Anita could see she was mouthing numbers, doing math in her head. "And what about the rest?"

"Ha'penny for the scones, one penny for the tarts? We haven't really settled it yet," Beatrice said as Cruella circled the desserts.

"That's quite the tidy profit," Cruella said, smirking.

Anita felt uneasy, and not just because she was nervous about Perdita. What did Cruella care about the profits? "It is a fundraiser, after all," Anita said. "We have to raise enough for our dues and supplies."

Another cry came from the cupboard. This time Cruella noticed.

"What was that?" she asked sharply.

"That was me," Madeline said, sniffling. Everyone, including Cruella, turned to look at her. Madeline was pretending to cry. "My parents are bakers, and this whole experience—it just gets me so emotional,

being in the kitchen again." She put her hand on her heart.

Cruella frowned. "That's very strange," she said. "Emotional over baking?" She shook her head. "Make sure you clean everything when you're done. I look forward to seeing the finished profits—I mean, finished products. Toodle-oo!" And with a wave, Cruella was gone.

The girls let out sighs of relief. Anita opened the cupboard and scooped up Perdita. "I'm so sorry for shoving you in there." Perdita licked her cheeks, letting her know she was forgiven.

"That Cruella is an odd duck," Madeline said.

"To be fair, you were the one crying over baking," Penelope said. Everyone laughed.

The Arties returned to their tasks, and soon the tense air from Cruella's visit was gone. Anita couldn't help worrying, though, underneath her smiles and laughter. At what point would it become impossible to keep Perdita hidden?

Chapter 7
The Escape

The next day, the Arties set up their cake stall in the great hall, and word soon spread through the usually silent school about the fresh sweet treats. Students and teachers alike showed up to purchase the goodies. The fundraiser lifted the spirits of everyone who stopped by. It was the first time Anita had seen that many smiles at Dahlington.

Over the following weeks, the Arties continued to spend time together. They planned fundraisers (all graciously approved by Cruella), worked on art projects with what limited supplies they could find around the school, studied together, and were always laughing. Classes were becoming more bearable as well. Her literature teacher even let the class make collages for one of their book reports. But the best parts of Anita's days were the ones she spent with Perdita. They'd play together with Anita's stuffed rabbit, cuddle as Anita sketched, or work on tricks to help with Perdita's obedience. She'd already learned to sit and roll over.

"Stay" was going to take more practice—and unfortunately, that was the command Anita most needed Perdita to learn.

No matter what she did, Anita couldn't figure out how to keep Perdita calm when she heard a loud noise outside. Beatrice had been kind enough to babysit Perdita whenever possible, even moving study dates with Elsie, a girl from her class, to do so. But the girls couldn't be with her all the time. Keeping the puppy a secret was becoming more and more difficult, especially during the hubbub of the Arties' weekend fundraisers.

After the cake stall, the girls held a car wash. While the Arties were outside, a honking horn set off Perdita in Anita's dorm. Anita had to run to her room to help Perdita quiet down before anyone discovered where the barks were coming from.

On another weekend, the Arties organized a scavenger hunt with the chance to win a new hat from Claire's father's shop. The students who signed up worked in teams of four to follow clues around the halls and grounds of Dahlington. It was the first time Anita had seen so many of her peers working and laughing together. But in the middle of overseeing the fun, Anita spotted the Dapperton boys beginning soccer practice down the road. She raced to her room just in time to catch Perdita before she started barking at the whistle.

By now, the Arties had almost enough money for their club dues and new art supplies. They decided to throw one final event to reach their goal. They set up an art fair that was open not just to Dahlington, but also to Dapperton and the local town. In the weeks leading up to the fair, Anita noticed people around her taking newfound pride in Dahlington's appearance. Teachers pitched in to tidy the classrooms. Janitors hauled paint from the basement to touch up the cracks. Anita even saw students straighten the odd crooked picture or plaque.

The Arties made paintings, crafts, bracelets, and other items to sell at the art fair. Anita was responsible for the raffle booth. The prize was a beautiful portrait she had painted of Perdita. The fair had just gotten underway, with the outside guests wandering into the great hall, as Anita set up the portrait on an easel for display.

"That's a beautiful picture," someone said.

Anita turned to see a sandy-haired boy admiring the painting of Perdita. He was dressed in a Dapperton uniform. "Thank you," she replied.

"My parents promised me I'd get a dog just like it for Christmas. A Dalmatian, right? Is she yours?" the boy asked.

"Um, she kind of is—yes, but—" Anita stammered.

"My name's Roger." The boy stuck out his hand. Anita reached to shake it, but before she could, a wailing alarm sounded from somewhere outside the school.

"What's that?" Anita asked, startled.

"That's just the alarm from the fire brigade." Roger gave Anita a funny look. "Don't worry. I don't think we're on fire." He chuckled.

"I have to check something," Anita said.

She hurried off toward the dormitories. Perdita was likely getting worked up into a frenzy.

But no sooner had Anita stepped outside than she saw a blur of black and white racing toward the road.

"Oh, no!" Anita shouted. She sprinted toward Perdita, who was running at top speed toward the alarm in the distance.

Beatrice appeared, chasing after Anita and Perdita. "I popped into the room to get more raffle tickets. The moment I opened the door, she bolted!" Beatrice shouted as she ran.

Perdita was scurrying fast on her tiny

legs. She let out a bark as she bounded down the school drive. Anita thanked her lucky stars that everyone was inside at the art fair.

Suddenly, from Anita's left, someone else dashed toward Perdita. It was Roger, the boy Anita had met moments earlier. He rounded down the driveway and managed to beat the puppy to the road, catching her as she ran by.

Roger held out the wriggling Perdita for Anita to take. "I think I recognize this little rascal from your painting."

Anita panted, trying to catch her breath. "Thank you, Roger. Oh, thank you."

Beatrice reached them next. "I'm so sorry, Anita! She was too fast!"

Roger ruffled the fur on top of Perdita's head and handed her to Anita. The fire alarm had faded, and Perdita was calming down. "How wonderful you're allowed to keep pets here," Roger said.

Beatrice and Anita exchanged glances. "We aren't exactly *allowed* to," Anita said. "Please don't mention this to anyone."

Roger clapped his hands together. "An undercover Dalmatian operation. That is exciting!"

Anita laughed. "Right now I wish it was

a little *less* exciting. I'd better get Perdita back to our room."

Beatrice turned to Roger. "And you're missing our fantastic art fair. Let me show you around," she said.

Anita bade Roger and her roommate goodbye and headed back toward the dorm with Perdita underneath her sweater. As she rounded the corner of the great hall, familiar black and white hair caught her attention. Cruella De Vil was rapping on the *staff only* entrance.

Anita ducked behind the wall and out of sight. In addition to giving permission for all the fundraisers, Cruella had also shown up at each one, with a peculiar interest in what the Arties were selling and how much money they were bringing in. Anita had supposed she just liked counting as much as she did creating bizarre fashions. She was curious, though, about what the older girl was up to, and she couldn't help peering around the corner to watch.

The staff door opened and the Headmistress appeared. The woman was sobbing, her shoulders hunched. She was holding a framed painting, but Anita

couldn't see the image. Cruella handed the Headmistress a large swath of fabric, and together they draped it over the frame. Then they went inside, closing the door behind them.

With the coast clear, Anita continued on to her dormitory. She couldn't make sense of what she had just seen. Was the Headmistress really *that* upset about keeping her belongings free of dust? If she was, why had she let the rest of Dahlington get so far into a state of disrepair?

Back in her room, Anita settled Perdita down and waited until the puppy fell asleep before she returned to the art fair. She soon forgot about the strange sighting of Cruella and the Headmistress, because her concern for her puppy was much greater. Anita didn't want to live her life in fear of Perdita's being discovered. Nor did she want Perdita to feel for her whole puppyhood like Anita had felt her first two weeks at Dahlington—like she couldn't be herself and couldn't feel truly at home. But what could Anita do? She couldn't stop sudden noises from happening, and she couldn't control her dog from afar. She had to find another solution.

And that was when Anita had an idea.

Chapter 8
The Clubhouse

Once the art fair was over, the Arties spent the afternoon cleaning up. As the girls packed away the few crafts that hadn't sold and Beatrice counted the money they'd made, Anita brought up her plan.

"Arties, I think I have an idea for two of the biggest problems facing our club," Anita said. "There's a place that could serve both as our clubhouse *and* as a permanent location to hide Perdita. Care to take a walk? I'll show you."

Beatrice checked her watch. "I was supposed to meet that girl, Elsie, from my English class to study. She's been asking me every weekend, but we've been so busy. And I can't imagine why she needs to study. She's got the best grade in the class!"

"Why don't you ask her to join the art club?" Madeline said.

"She doesn't want to! She's afraid or something." Beatrice shrugged. "Anyway, Arties come first. Let's see your idea, Anita."

Anita led her friends across the school

grounds to the run-down equipment shed where she'd found Perdita weeks earlier.

The Arties looked skeptically at the shed.

"You want this to be our clubhouse?" Penelope asked, reaching out to open the door, but the handle fell to the ground at her touch.

"It doesn't look like much now, but think about it," Anita said, hoping her excitement would catch on. "The janitors keep extra paint in the basement. There are old cleaning supplies already inside. With some hard work, we could make this our meeting place *and* a house for Perdita. No one would hear her playing, howling, or barking."

"I'm willing to try," Madeline said. "For Perdita, at the very least."

"For Perdita!" the rest of the girls cheered.

The next day, the Arties returned to the equipment shed with Perdita and got to work. First they cleaned out all the rubbish. The shed was full of relics from the school's past, from old jerseys to dusty history textbooks to battered trophies. It was fun going through the old stuff. Even Perdita was having a good time, with an endless supply of old balls to play with.

"What's this?" Beatrice asked, holding up a pennant in the school's colors of maroon and gold. It said *Dahlington*, and there was an outline of a long funny-looking dog on the banner as well.

"Look—this has it, too!" Lucy cried. She held up a hockey stick with the same dog image painted on the handle.

"This too," Claire said, as she popped on a maroon cap with a gold dog on it.

"There's a spider on that," Penelope said. Claire shrieked and threw the hat from her head. The other girls erupted into laughter. Then they all got back to cleaning, keeping a lookout for more dog images.

Finally, after a weekend of hard work,

the shed looked identical to the one in the old tennis club photo. The trim was painted a cheery aqua, the siding a crisp white, and the door a bold red. Inside, the colors were blues and reds and pinks, as well as natural brown for the wood. It was the perfect place for an art club—and a perfect house for a Dalmatian puppy.

Anita arranged a finishing touch: a vase of wildflowers on a small table the girls had rescued from the rubble. As she stepped back to admire the clubhouse, her new friends applauded.

"Why are you cheering?" Anita asked.

"Without you," Beatrice started, "we

might all still be miserable and lonely."

"The art club has been my favorite part of Dahlington," Madeline said.

"Same here," the other girls echoed.

Anita beamed. "There's still one problem, though."

"What's that?" Lucy asked.

"We aren't an official club!" Anita said. "At least not in the eyes of Dahlington Academy."

"We have everything we need now," Beatrice said. "The funds, the members, the meeting place . . ."

"Should we make it official?" Anita asked her friends.

"Yes!" the other girls cried. Perdita woofed.

"I'll go make the request with the Headmistress," Anita said. "Beatrice, do you have the cashbox? Would you like to come along?"

Beatrice checked her watch. "Yes," she said, "but I have to meet Elsie. I've broken our appointments too many times." Beatrice handed Anita the cashbox with their saved club dues. "I'll meet you back here afterward?"

Anita nodded. She addressed the other Arties. "Please keep an eye on Perdita, and wish me luck!"

Chapter 9
Making It Official

Anita knocked on the Headmistress's office door.

To Anita's surprise, Cruella appeared. She eyed the cashbox in Anita's hands. "Anita, darling. Is that what I think it is?"

"Yep! We're ready to make the club official," Anita said. "Can I speak to the Headmistress?"

Cruella slipped out of the office and

into the hallway, closing the door behind her. "The Headmistress is very busy at the moment," she whispered. She looked back at the cashbox. "May I see?"

Anita handed over the box. Cruella opened it and counted the money.

"Here are our application form and signatures." Anita handed over both documents to Cruella.

"Everything appears to be in order." Cruella's lips curled into a wry smile. She withdrew an official-looking certificate from inside her velvet overcoat and handed it to Anita.

"It says 'Official Dahlington Academy Art

Official Dahlington Academy Art Club

Club,'" Anita read aloud. "You had this all ready to go?"

"I never doubted you for a moment, Anita darling," Cruella said. "I knew you'd make this happen for me. I mean, you. Your new club."

Anita scratched her head. "So the Headmistress has authorized the club? I don't need to speak to her?"

"I briefed her," Cruella said. "She's very pleased you've taken this on. As am I. It's going to be wonderful for the fashion club."

"Don't you mean wonderful to have an art club?" Anita asked.

Cruella paused. "Did I say wonderful for the fashion club? I just meant wonderful to have another club in the mix." Cruella cackled and clutched the cashbox. "I'll go take this to the treasury for safekeeping. Toodles, Anita!"

"Thank you!" Anita said as Cruella disappeared into the Headmistress's office. Cruella was definitely a strange girl. But Anita had to admit that she'd been nothing but helpful.

Anita headed back to the equipment shed, feeling lighter than air. She thought about the afternoon a couple of months prior when a much lonelier girl opened a letter from her mum and got the idea to join a club. Since then, so much had changed. Anita had created her own sense of home at Dahlington. And it made her feel strong.

Anita's daydreaming was interrupted by the other Arties running toward her, Beatrice leading the way.

"Anita!" Beatrice huffed and puffed, trying to catch her breath.

"Did you already hand over our dues?" Madeline asked. The Arties all looked worried and frantic.

"Yes . . ." Anita said slowly. She held up the official club certificate.

"Oh, no," Lucy said, putting her head in her hands.

"What is it?" Anita asked.

"The reason Elsie kept wanting to see me wasn't to study. It was to tell me about what really happened with all the other clubs," Beatrice said. "It was Cruella! She used her influence with the Headmistress to get them shut down. She found all these supposed rules they broke. Sabotaged them. One by one."

"But why would she do that?" Anita asked.

"Think about it," Claire said. "Once the other clubs were shut down, there was only one club left—one club that could use all the funding for itself."

"She took the other clubs' money for the fashion club," Anita said, piecing it together.

"That's how she's paying for all that expensive fabric and those fancy sewing machines," Lucy explained.

It all made sense to Anita now: Cruella's special interest in their fundraising. The glee in her eyes when she saw the money in the cashbox. "And we just handed her our money," Anita said in horror.

"We have to try to stop her!" Penelope cried.

The Arties' eyes met. "Let's go," Anita said. And they ran to the Headmistress's office to try to catch Cruella.

Chapter 10
Confronting Cruella

The Arties burst into the Headmistress's office without knocking. The Headmistress was seated behind her desk. Next to her stood Cruella, cashbox in hand.

"Whatever she's saying, it's not true!" Beatrice shouted.

"This is the club you've been telling me about?" the Headmistress asked Cruella.

"They're simply out of control," the

older girl said. "They can't be trusted as representatives of Dahlington Academy in an official club capacity."

The Arties gasped. "How dare you," Claire said, seething.

"You see what I mean." Cruella smirked. "There is, at the very least, a behavior issue."

"Young ladies," the Headmistress said, "Cruella has notified me that your art club was formed as an excuse to break rules and disrupt the school order. Is this true?"

"I assure you that's not the case," Anita said. "We just want to have an art club.

And we haven't broken any rules. All of our fundraisers were approved."

"But I did not approve any such events," the Headmistress said.

"Cruella did," Penelope said. "As your student aide."

Cruella put her hand to her chest in surprise. "Of course that can't be true. I don't have the authority to approve things on the Headmistress's behalf." She snorted, as though what Penelope had just said was ridiculous.

The Arties exchanged horrified looks. Cruella had been setting them up all along!

Anita tried to compose herself. "It seems

there has been a miscommunication, ma'am. We will certainly seek your permission *directly*"—she glared at Cruella as she said this—"in the future."

"Unfortunately, that won't undo the numerous conduct rules they've broken," Cruella told the Headmistress.

"Conduct rules? Like what?" Lucy asked.

"Why, all the unauthorized behavior: engaging in for-profit activities on campus, stealing from the kitchen pantries, fraternizing with members of the boys' academy." Cruella rattled off the list as the Arties glanced at each other nervously. "And of course, making hideous paintings they try to pass off as *art* when in fact we have actual art on campus in the form of my brilliant fashions." Cruella tossed her black and white hair and snorted again, dramatically.

"Cruella," the Headmistress said wearily, "creating art you may not like is not a breach of conduct."

"Well, it ought to be," Cruella said, sneering.

The Headmistress rubbed her temples. "Girls, you all seem like lovely students. We can't have rampant rule breaking, of course, but, Cruella"—the Headmistress turned to her aide—"it also sounds like these girls were under the impression they had proper permission. I'm not sure disbanding the club is what we should do about their first violation."

Cruella rolled her eyes. Then she reached into a pocket of her long velvet coat and withdrew a small metal cylinder. A devilish grin spread across her face. "First violation, you say?" Anita watched her put the object to her lips and blow. For a moment, nothing happened.

Then the unmistakable sound of a dog barking reached the office. Anita realized, too late, that Cruella had blown a dog whistle. She tried to contain her panic as the barks grew louder and louder.

"Is that a dog I hear?" the Headmistress asked.

The barking was getting closer. Anita heard claws scraping the marble floor in the hallway outside, and her heart fell into her stomach. Finally: *boom*. The door burst open, and Perdita bounded into the Headmistress's office.

"*Woof!*" Perdita barked, as if she was announcing her arrival. She leapt into Anita's arms, licking her in happiness, so excited to have been summoned.

"Hello, sweet girl," Anita whispered to her pet, her voice breaking.

"Headmistress," Cruella said, pointing at the pair, "Anita and her club of cronies have been hiding this contraband creature for weeks, right under your nose."

Anita held her puppy, breathing in the scent of the animal she loved so much. Everyone else in the room was quiet, including the Headmistress.

Cruella chuckled mercilessly at Anita. "You thought you were doing such a good job keeping her hidden. Please." She turned to the Headmistress. "Ma'am, I apologize on behalf of these hooligans.

I should have done more to rein them in."

The Arties looked on in shock. The Headmistress rose from her desk.

"Could you put the animal down, please?" the Headmistress asked.

Anita set Perdita on the floor. The Headmistress crouched to look at the puppy. Perdita ran forward to greet her, sniffing the Headmistress's shoes.

Then the Headmistress scooped Perdita up, drew her in close, and cooed: "Oh, you pwecious widdle thing! Who's a good girl? Adorable widdle cutie-wutie pupper. *You* are!"

The Arties gaped in surprise. Cruella flared her nostrils in disgust.

As the Headmistress cuddled Perdita, she gave Cruella an order. "Take them down."

Cruella began to protest. "But, Headmistress, remember—"

"Take them down, Cruella." The Headmistress's voice was firm.

Cruella nodded, reluctant but obedient. She pulled the fabric covering from the large piece of artwork on the wall closest to her. As the fabric fell to the floor, the painting underneath was revealed. It was a large oil portrait of a very distinguished, very handsome dachshund.

Chapter 11
Henry

Cruella walked around the room, yanking the fabric coverings from the furniture, the lamps, and the rest of the artwork. With every reveal came another sighting of the dachshund: embroidered pillows featuring his face, a lamp with a bronze dachshund as its base and floppy ears dangling from the shade, photographs of the Headmistress and the dachshund together, needlework hangings with phrases such as "Happy Dachshund, Happy Dahlington" on the wall. Everywhere Anita looked in the office was a dachshund.

When Cruella was finished, she threw all the fabric into a pile in the corner and folded her arms. The Headmistress handed Perdita back to Anita and went to an oil painting of the Headmistress holding the dachshund.

"This is Henry," she began. "At the beginning of last school year, he passed away." She touched her palm to the dog's face. "Henry was our school mascot. When he was alive, we were the Dahlington Dachshunds." The Headmistress pointed to

another wall hanging. It was a pennant like the one the girls had found when they were cleaning out the equipment shed: the outline of a dachshund prancing next to *Dahlington* in gold letters on maroon felt. Anita understood now why the discarded pieces of sports equipment had the same dog on them. It was Henry!

The Headmistress continued. "Henry was also my companion for seventeen years." Her face was full of sorrow. "After he died, I couldn't bear to look at anything that reminded me of him. It caused me too much pain. That included everything in here and, unfortunately, the school itself. I admit I've let the buildings fall into disrepair." She gestured to Cruella. "Cruella offered to hide Henry's image for me so I would be less sad. I also instituted stricter rules, thinking that would keep things in line while I was grieving. Cruella stepped in as my student aide to help." The Headmistress looked at Cruella. "But it seems Cruella may have taken the role of *aide* a bit too far."

Cruella lifted her nose into the air.

"I take responsibility for all of that," the Headmistress said. "But, Anita, it's important you understand that keeping a pet on campus without permission is against the rules here at Dahlington."

"I understand, Headmistress," Anita said, bowing her head.

The Headmistress set a hand on Anita's shoulder. "I should have set a better example. I didn't know how to find my way out of my grief. But now"—the woman beamed at Perdita—"seeing this  magnificent young creature . . . What's her name?"

"Perdita," Anita answered.

"Instead of being a reminder of the pain

of losing Henry, Perdita has brought back that great feeling of love that can only come from a dog." The Headmistress reached out to pet Perdita again. The puppy licked her hand in response. "Anita, Perdita will not only be welcome here at Dahlington for as long as you're a student, but in fact, I think she should become our new mascot. The *Dahlington Dalmatians*!"

The Arties cheered.

"Also," the Headmistress continued, "the art club will stay an official Dahlington club. And I promise I'll look into the other clubs that may have been . . . lost over the past year."

"That would be amazing!" Anita

exclaimed. She couldn't believe the news. Perdita would not only be living out in the open—she'd be celebrated!

Cruella huffed loudly and stomped out of the office.

"She'll be okay," the Headmistress said. "Cruella has a bit of a flair for the dramatic."

"I'll say," Penelope muttered.

"Stick around for a moment, girls," the Headmistress said. "I may have some of Henry's old toys here."

The art club stayed in the Headmistress's office for a while longer, hearing stories of Henry's glory days, looking at his many photos, and discussing plans for Perdita, including a debut ceremony that would be a fun event for the entire school. The Headmistress also tasked the art club with designing a new school pennant for the Dahlington Dalmatians. The Arties were delighted to accept.

Later, Anita, Beatrice, Penelope, Claire, Lucy, and Madeline left the office with Perdita following close behind. To their surprise, Cruella was waiting for them.

"Uh-oh," Beatrice groaned.

"I suppose I should offer you congratulations," Cruella said. "The role of mascot is pretty important. If you ever need someone to dog-sit or take her for a walk, I can help with that." Cruella tried to smile at Perdita, but it looked more like she was baring her teeth.

"No way!" Claire whispered harshly at Anita.

"That's very kind of you, Cruella," Anita said. "But I can handle her on my own."

"Whatever you say, darling." Cruella shrugged. "But there's no reason why we can't continue being pals, despite a little friendly competition with the clubs and all."

Anita swallowed. *Friendly competition?*

"Pals?" Madeline asked.

Anita remembered how lonely she'd been at the beginning of the school year. Perhaps Cruella's behavior came from her own source of loneliness. Or maybe she just liked being cruel. Either way, Anita couldn't bear to turn down someone who was looking for a friend.

"Why don't we take it one step at a time, Cruella?" Anita offered. "You could join the art club."

"She can?" Penelope asked.

"Fashion is a form of art, after all," Anita said.

Cruella made a face like she smelled something bad. But she said, "Fine. I'll join your club."

"Great," Anita said. She ignored the glares from her fellow Arties. She'd explain to them another time. Either Cruella needed a friend, in which case the art club should be kind to her, or she was an enemy, in which case the art club should keep her close.

"I will, however," Cruella said, "insist on designing our club uniforms, which we desperately need."

"We can put that to a vote," Beatrice said.

"I know how I'm going to vote," Penelope grumbled.

"We'll discuss it at our next meeting," Anita said, "where we'll start working on our Dahlington Dalmatian creations."

"Should we start with an illustration?" asked Claire.

"That's my nomination," said Madeline.

"Something to look forward to, after all our trials and tribulations," Beatrice added.

"It will be a sensation!" Lucy said with a giggle.

"Worth a standing ovation!" Penelope cheered.

"I think my membership is going to be on a trial basis," Cruella interjected, rolling her eyes.

The Arties made their way back to the dormitories. Students grinned and pointed at Perdita as they walked past. Some even asked to meet her. Anita smiled as Perdita brought joy to everyone she encountered.

It seemed that Dahlington, just as much
as Anita herself, had simply needed a
Dalmatian.